One or Two Steps Only

Sean Reagan

Copyright © 2014 Sean Reagan

Quotes from A Course in Miracles are taken from versions in the public domain.

All rights reserved. No part of this book may be used or reproduced in any manner whatsoever without written permission.

First Printing, June 2014
ISBN-13: *978-1499694222*

Published by *Sean Reagan*
seanreagan.com

One or Two Steps Only

SEAN REAGAN

CONTENTS

Preface	1
First Steps	4
Separation	11
The Safety of God Is	26
Becoming Foolish	34
How Simple the Solution Is	40
The Infinite Patience of the Holy Spirit	48
The Given	54
On Mistakes and Forgiveness	61
On Seeing Differently	68
A Focus On How	74
Beyond What Can Be Taught	78
On Choosing Inner Peace	86
A Loving Yes	90

PREFACE TO THE FIRST EDITION

I remember in Kindergarten - five years old - Mrs. Gould pulled me aside and showed me a book. It was about a goat named Billy who was climbing a hill. The illustrations were charcoal, the sentences short and simple.

Mrs. Gould showed me how to sound out the words. It made me very happy - blissfully happy, actually - for reasons that were then obscure to me. That book was probably twenty pages long and my life changed before we were halfway through it. I became obsessed with words and the sounds they made. *Obsessed*. And I have never stopped being obsessed. Reading, writing, talking . . . I'll stay just this side of Heaven for a good book, a rich sentence, a revelatory poem.

I began writing about *A Course in Miracles* about ten minutes after I started reading it and all these many years later, I have not stopped. There is nothing mystical about it. It is just what I do - because it is fun, because I can, because it's a part of how I learn and because I meet helpful and interesting people. Why else do something?

This little book is not offered from the high towers of wisdom nor the mystical vales of insight. I think of myself as a serious student of *A Course in Miracles*, and I think of *A Course in Miracles* as that expression of the perennial philosophy that resonates most clearly and fruitfully within me. All I do is witness to what happens along the way. If you're reading this, I'm grateful to share the path a while. If it's helpful, fantastic. If not, no hard feelings. Take everything with a grain of salt, and keep the shaker handy. I'm figuring it out as I go, same as you are.

Most of these essays started out as blog posts at my website seanreagan.com. The questions and answers that follow some of the essays are either taken from commentary on that blog or private correspondence or - in one case - a recorded dialogue from an ACIM study group. I have whittled the questions down considerably and taken great liberties in the composition of my answers to hopefully make them coherent and intelligent. I hope they shed some light on the essays.

You know, that first time I was taught how language worked – given a glimpse of the universe, really - I asked Mrs. Gould if I could stay inside and read. I skipped a couple of recesses that day, which was a big deal, because I loved being outside. I hated school generally, and always availed myself of any opportunity (both licit and illicit) to be out-of-doors. I am sure she was surprised and delighted. How grateful I was - and remain - for her "yes."

I sensed that day that I had found my life's work, such as it was, and such as you can sense such things when you're a child, and I attended to it the only way I knew: all in, nothing held back. I approach *A Course in Miracles* that way too, though I've slowed down a bit with age. Full-tilt is not the right way to be an ACIM student and it's certainly not the only way but it has been a useful way for me. It has worked for me. There is such a thing as a peace and joy that surpasses understanding and we are it. The course will teach us that in a practical way if we are ready. I tell people to give themselves to it, as much as they can, as far as they can, and let it work on them. What else is there?

I am grateful to all my teachers - and to the brothers and sisters who share the way with me in varied forms. So many beautiful lights! We are never lost, never bereft. And thank you, my friend - reading in a time and space apparently apart from that in which I write. I take as fact our togetherness, and offer these words in that spirit. For a little while - one or two steps only - we may lift each other. For a little while we may know in one another home.

FIRST STEPS

I wonder sometimes what I would have done had *A Course in Miracles* not showed up in my life when it did. All the spiritual paths with which I was familiar no longer worked. It felt as though I had walked for days and nights through an enormous desert only to discover another desert. I was tired and discouraged. I was lonely.

Often, it is only when we exhaust all our apparent options and reach the limits of our own effort, that life will finally offer us its beneficence and clarity. This is not a condition but a fact: when we drop our own efforts and ideas and busy-ness, the pure action of life is what remains. But we must come to the wisdom of doing nothing. For most of us, this is not easy. It takes a long time and a lot of learning before we can see *what is*. Lifetimes, perhaps.

The blessing of *A Course in Miracles* was instantly present in my life. The first few months of my study were blissful and energetic. A space of which I had long been unaware was revealed. I began to perceive, however dimly, the truth of "nothing real can be threatened." My thinking began to shift away from the body and its survival and towards eternal values.

A Course in Miracles meets us where we are, and gives as much help and direction as we are capable of receiving in a given moment. It is a force of energy that is available to us, but we have to ask. We have to be open. And not everyone is ready.

I cannot say whether *A Course in Miracles* is your path, but if it is - if you have made that decision - then I think it merits your full attention, your full devotion, and all of the intensity that you can muster. It has the capacity to awaken you to your natural relationship with God. But it asks for your awareness. It asks that you make it your practice. It asks these things. It doesn't demand them. And if it is for you, then you have to answer it. Your life becomes the answer.

The course, because it reflects the Voice of God, requires an answer. It will not accept anything less because what we are in truth will not accept anything less. As soon as we make space for it – however unconsciously, however unwillingly – it becomes a subtle but persistent presence. It asks us to be in relationship with it and, through it, in relationship with God. This is very personal and nobody can decide or do it for you. The call is unique, tailored to your life as you understand and experience it. Only you can hear it. And only you can respond.

The truth is that we are lost and broken. We

are confused. These are the facts of our lives. All of us. We do not recognize the truth and we are always going to go looking for it tomorrow. Confusion and delay attend our every move, shade our every word. To deny or justify this fact is to evade our responsibility for discovering what we are in truth and thus ending confusion *now*. Nobody else can do it. Not Jesus, not the Buddha. Not a priest or a therapist. Not a spouse or a lover or a best friend. We wander through our lives and through the world without noticing the great beauty and wisdom that naturally grounds and envelopes us. A divine energy – eternal and infinite – infuses life, from the human being to the flower, from the whale to the chickadee, from a single blade of grass to the moon, and we drift past it in sleep, altogether unaware. Creation is ours and we turn away. We are bereft in the midst of abundance.

This is the choice we make! We are given the gift of life and we squander it. And on what? Trinkets and baubles to adorn our bodies, money to fill our bank accounts, accomplishments to feed our fragile egos. We all do it. We have been doing it for a long time. We are scared to die because we don't know what it means to live. And we don't know what it means to live because we don't know what we are in truth. In the face of this we become busy, like mice frantically grooming in the shadow of hungry snakes. We don't know where to go so we go in circles and call it progress, call it improvement, call it a spiritual journey.

A Course in Miracles comes along at this time and in this place – it comes to us personally, meeting us where we are - and it offers us a way to learn who we are. It offers us a way out of the vicious circle in which we live. It asks questions of us: who walks beside you? Whose kingdom is the world for you today? Do you want to be happy or do you want to be right?

Most of us read those questions and keep going because we aren't really interested in answers or solutions. We are interested in getting something, in getting along. We think that inner peace and joy are rewards that we will get for doing the lessons and reading the text. We rush through it – giving only part of our attention, letting things slip around the edges - because we are not interested in awakening but in our ideas about awakening, our ideal of awakening. And that is why we never wake up. That is why our loneliness and grief continue unabated. We have only ourselves to blame but to see this fact clearly would require that we accept responsibility for our condition. And it is so much easier to blame what is external – our parents, our teachers, our politicians, the economy. The world exists that we might not turn within and encounter what is responsible for joy and inner peace. We consent to suffer and pretend to be surprised and disappointed when - day after day, year after year, lifetime after lifetime – we suffer.

So we have to ask ourselves if we are ready. We have to ask if we are ready to ask questions and give attention to the answers. Serious attention, sustained attention. The answers are given but hearing them is not easy, because we are so distracted and goal-oriented. We are so casual and half-hearted. Our wanting results impedes our capacity to hear. It always has. Two thousand years ago when Jesus offered his teachings to those who had ears to hear he was not talking about the appendages on either side of our head. He knew what he was dealing with. He had to deal with it in himself in order to become the Christ. We all do.

If we are serious about *A Course in Miracles*, then we will make a space in our life for it. This means that we will simplify our lives and bring them to order so that our practice of the course will become central, will become our ground. The decision to do this is internal. We are no longer going to be casual and relaxed. We are not going to try and bring the word of God down to our level, twist it to satisfy our shallow wants and petty desires. We don't have to know in advance what the alternative to littleness is; we just have to be ready to welcome it. We have to be ready to say, not my will but Your Will be done. I will not want anything other than what God wills for me today. What power those words have! When we utter them, life shifts to accommodate our decision. If we truly believed that *A Course in Miracles* was the word of God - that it could deliver us to "awareness of perfect Oneness and the knowledge that there is nothing else" and thus awaken us from the grim slumber of illusion and death - an hour a day wouldn't be enough. We would give every minute of every day to it. Whether we were cooking or teaching or changing diapers or doing yoga, we would be focused on hearing the word of God and bringing it into application. And yet we can barely muster fifteen or twenty minutes. And sometimes we forget even that much.

So we have to decide to change that. We have to refuse to accept our mediocrity. What made Jesus the Christ is here for us too, and if we say yes to it, if we follow and give attention to it, then we too will know that peace and that happiness. We will know it because we *are* it. That is what we will remember.

If we are clear in our intention, and humble in our recognition of our need for help, then the day will be given to us in order that we might remember our Oneness with God. The way to this remembrance will open naturally, without any effort on our part. Our part is simply to follow as the path reveals itself. Have you ever watched ducklings swimming after their mother? How naturally they fall into place – no questions, no angst, no negotiations? Of course we are not ducks but that doesn't mean we can't also be that obedient, that willing, that faithful. What does it cost a baby duck to be a baby duck? Do you really think that it takes more for you to be you? All that is required is that we make the choice for God - that we be *willing* to make the choice. And everything else follows. Everything else flows.

We can complicate this, of course. We have gotten very good at complication and obfuscation. There is no clarity that we cannot tie up in knots or hide beneath veils. That is the nature of mind at the shallow level of the ego: that is its defense system against truth and love. Make it difficult: make it complicated: make it confusing. And do it in a way that allows us to pretend we're not responsible. *We* aren't making life difficult – we are simply seeing the truth that life itself is difficult. It's just a fact, not a decision that we make. That's what we want to say because it absolves us of responsibility. But God is as clear and perfect as a ray of sunlight. No matter what our minds do to that beam of light – put it in a poem, measure or harness it, take a nap in it or lay out a picnic in it - the fact of its perfection and presence remains. The grass grows and the flowers open and the bees flutter by and the sea sparkles. The truth is true: it is not up for a vote. It is unaffected by our ideas about it. God *is*.

We are so scared of that! We are scared to know God, scared to know ourselves, and scared to do any of the work that is involved in coming to that knowledge. But our fear has only the power we give it. *A Course in Miracles* meets us precisely where we are and undoes our fear, undoes our unwillingness, and restores to our awareness the knowledge that God is Love and we are one with God. If we give our attention to the course - its lessons, its questions and answers, its logic and poetry, all of it - then the false self of substitution will be gently and surely set aside in favor of what we are in truth. And what remains will be what has been since before time began and will remain long after it is forgotten: the radiant, unencumbered and limitless presence of God: our only home, our only peace, our only joy.

SEPARATION

You wonder sometimes what the separation from God is, and why it is our condition, or seems to be, and what life will look or feel like when it ends. It's a good question. Our separation from God is what we are trying to solve, or resolve. Or dissolve maybe. When that separation ends, the journey ends too. Our long sufferance is diffused into joy.

The temptation in talking about separation is to regurgitate the mythology of *A Course in Miracles*. You know – the tiny mad idea at which we forgot to laugh. But that's tricky, because we always want to take that story literally. Or else we get bogged down in its metaphysics – how can what is one have an idea that is not shared by what else is one? And so forth. Either way it's like wading through heavy mud.

Literal translations of what are simply meant to be helpful stories, and metaphysical obfuscation, are really just tools for keeping salvation far away and inaccessible. We have to move beyond them, which is to say that we have to take ourselves more seriously.

A Course in Miracles says that we are "at home in God, dreaming of exile, but perfectly capable of awakening to reality."

That is a nice image: we are asleep in heaven, dreaming we are in hell. In that case, all that one has to do is wake up from the dream. There's nothing to be done in the dream itself. The dream is the level of illusion. The cause of awakening does not reside there.

> The Son is the effect, whose Cause he would deny. And so he seems to *be* the cause, producing real effects. Nothing can have effects without a cause, and to confuse the two is merely to fail to understand them both.

If we could see the truth of this, it would instantly liberate us: we live in the dream of separation and there is nothing inside that dream that can end it. There really is nothing that we can do. The effective action takes place at another level, internally. There are other powers, other energies. To avail ourselves of them is to avail ourselves of God, and of Truth as God created it, and when we do that, something happens. Cause and effect are restored to their proper places. What is true is known as true, and what is illusory is known as false. That is the ground of liberation. That is the clarity that allows us to remember God.

At some point, human beings - or consciousness, if you like - began a sort of unhelpful digression. We differentiated ourselves from our environment: the flowers, the trees, the buffalo, the people, the stars. We decided all that was "out there" and that we were its perceptive center. If you give a little attention to how your thoughts work, how they respond to the perceptions of your body's senses, then you will see that this is still true. There are two things that follow from this sense of self as a center of perception, this dot from which the whole world – indeed, the whole universe- radiates. The first is that it makes us feel special, almost god-like. And the second is that it makes us feel fearful. So we begin to feel both entitled and a little defensive. We want more. And we want better. And we want also to be protected. We want to be defended.

Wherever you perceive division – between you and the blue jays at the feeder, between the feeder and the blue jays, between the blue jays and the chickadees - understand that it originates in your thought. It is thought that separates maple trees from birch trees, Hindus from Catholics, and Iranians from Canadians. In reality, the world is much more in the nature of many shades of being merging into one. It is a dynamic flux. But we resist that oneness, that movement. We choose this or that element and tease it apart from the whole. When you do that over and over, with a thousand times ten thousand things, then eventually you lose the whole altogether. You forget it's even there.

The first time we did this, it probably had to do with convenience. Somebody wanted to distinguish between the berries that you could eat and the ones that killed you. It makes sense.

Unfortunately, this habit of separation or fragmentation didn't end there. It kept going, applying itself to everything that fell into its range of perception. There was no discernment, no balance, no reflection. It became our default mode because we never questioned it. What happens is that we start to take these divisions we are making more seriously than convenience mandates. We think because we're doing it then it must be important. It worked with the berries so we keep doing it. But just because it makes sense with berries or making fire or whatnot, doesn't mean its application should keep on extending to literally everything. But we never checked thought, in the sense of seeing its limitations. So we end up with separate countries and separate religions and we think it makes sense. We think they are real – not just ideas. It's the same thing with class divisions in society and divisions within the family and between races and genders. These are not real - they cause us all kinds of grief and sorrow and conflict – and we never see that they all begin and are sustained by thought. Wherever you look in the world, whatever you think, it is all reflective of this system of thought that is powerful, dysfunctional and in denial about what it is doing and how it works.

Primarily, of course, we have separated ourselves – from each other and from our true nature. We stand alone in terms of others and we stand divided with respect to creation. And the problem with that is that being alone that way is dishonest and illusory. At the ontological level, it is utterly terrifying. And it is way less satisfying than being one with stars and tulips and sleepy babies and turtles sunning themselves on logs and all of that. In a way, we set our tiny selves up as rulers only to learn that we had given up the only Kingdom there is. And so we are miserable and we are wracked with fear. God must hate us. God must want revenge.

But rather than face his fear and dissatisfaction directly and re-embrace Oneness, we double down on separation. We continue to deny reality and we begin to project our fear outside us, out there. This is the ego, the false self that insists on its specialness and opposes God and thus anchors our separation. The ego is the self that emerges after you participate in enough separation-thinking. You forget what's real and you're left with this shadow self that is built on projection and fear. It's like a robot running the same hopeless operating system in a loop.

A Course in Miracles says that "[e]xclusion and separation are synonymous . . . We have said before that the separation was and is dissociation, and that once it occurs projection becomes its main defense, or the device that keeps it going."

This dissociation inevitably leads to conflict. We want to become better than what was One - stronger, faster, smarter, bigger, more powerful. We want to triumph over what we had abandoned. And we want to defend ourselves against any possible retribution. We think big but we secretly fear we're small and so we're always on defense. Thus, we begin to concentrate on improving ourselves: our appearance, our belief systems, our weapons, our medicine, our stories. What is wrong is always out there. We are always blaming what is external. Yet *A Course in Miracles* teaches that this cannot work.

> What you project you disown, and therefore do not believe is yours. You are excluding yourself by the very judgment that you are different from the one on whom you project . . . projection will always hurt you. It reinforces your belief in your own split mind . . .

Do you see what is happening? The focus is not on being – not on truth as God created it - but on becoming, becoming something *other* than truth as God created it. And that is how the idea of psychological time was made and sustained: one needed a future into which one could project their imminent perfection and a past at which they could look back on and judge as "less than." I'm a better student than I was last year and in two years I'll be enlightened. That sort of thing.

This happened. We did this. And projection became our default mode of perception. And time just kept on segmenting. This is how the course can say that the separation "occurred over millions of years," and suggest that the atonement may take even longer.

In time, we forgot that the separation was simply a decision that we made - a way of thinking that was at odds with reality. Oneness became the dimmest of dim memories, a state that belonged only to rare human beings who had attained superhuman spiritual insights. We made God cruel and indifferent. And as our anguish and guilt predictably deepened, we passed in on to the external world through projection. The problem was never within us - it was never our mode of perception - but always some imperfection or flaw in the external world.

And in a way, this worked. We built bigger and better cities. We beat back plagues and infant mortality rates. We tripled our life spans. We crossed the ocean and flew to the moon. We invented money and six-string guitars and representative democracy and water purification filters and cheese-flavored popcorn. On the surface of it, there is so much for which to be grateful!

But of course we remain broken. We remain miserable and unsatisfied. The "God-shaped hole" that Sartre (and others) noticed yawns wider and wider. We yearn for inner peace. All this might be very subtle, barely noticeable, but it is there. It is the essence of our human condition. Deep down we sense we are as grand as moonlight, as deep as the sea, as strong as a mountain, and yet our lives appear to be a brief and painful struggle with suffering until we admit defeat and die into darkness . . .

What is whole has everything and so never knows yearning. But what is separated from wholeness knows only lack and scarcity. That is the condition of those who sleep and dream of hell. That is the itch we gave birth to eons ago and have never managed to scratch. And it will only get worse.

We have tried education but all that learning has not saved us. We are smart but we are hardly wise. Five hundred years ago we killed each other with axes and clubs and now we have nuclear weapons - we can eliminate all life forever - and we call it progress. We call it safety. Where is the wisdom in that?

We tried wealth but that hasn't worked. The emptiness we are talking about cannot be filled with fancy cars and elaborate houses and designer label clothing. Saving for retirement won't restore wholeness. We still hurt each other. We still gorge on food we don't need. Money brings out the worst in us, not what is wise.

And even religion has failed us. Jesus said two thousand years ago that "the kingdom of God is at hand" and "love they neighbor as thyself" and where are we? Twenty five hundred years of Buddha, two thousand of Jesus, five hundred years since the enlightenment, a century and a half of Thoreau, fifty years of Gandhi and Martin Luther King . . . where are we?

Part of coming to terms with the separation from God is accepting that there is no external system that is going to save us. Not *A Course in Miracles*, not the law of attraction, not a rigorous study of Plato or Wittgenstein or whomever. We have to see this. We have to see that if we are really going to undo the separation then are going to have to go beyond systems. We build these systems with the separated mind and all they beget is more separation. So they can't help anymore. None of them can.

I think you and I can see this if we look closely

One or Two Steps Only

at what we call life and don't shy away from what is uncomfortable or scary.

The separation is really no more than a habitual mode of thinking that privileges the egoic (or artificial) self over Oneness. It is a way of thinking that manages to screw everything up while simultaneously denying that it's doing anything. The problem is always out there: if we could only elect a different politician, or persuade people to become voluntarily poor, or stop eating meat, or become celibate, or follow Jesus . . .

This is why the course says over and over that salvation is literally nothing more than the recognition that we are doing all of this to ourselves.

> The secret to salvation is but this: That you are doing this unto yourself. No matter what the form of the attack, this is still true. Whoever takes the role of enemy and of attacker, still is this the truth. Whatever seems to be the cause of any pain and suffering you feel, this is still true. For you would not react at all to figures in a dream you knew that you were dreaming. Let them be as hateful and as vicious as they may, they could have no effect on you unless you failed to recognize it is your dream.

Those are powerful words! Salvation is the return to wholeness. It is the end of separation. It is literally a shift in thinking, a new paradigm in the structure and movement of thought. And we can do it.

If you look at the workbook lessons of *A Course in Miracles*, they are almost never taxing or demanding. You don't have to crawl across cut glass. You don't have to stay in one position for six hours. You don't have to tithe or cut off your hands or confess all your supposed sins. You simply have to devote some consistent time and energy to a shift in your thinking.

> The purpose of the workbook is to train your mind in a systematic way to a different perception of everyone and everything in the world. The exercises are planned to help you generalize the lessons, so that you will understand that each of them is equally applicable to everyone and everything you see.

The course insists that there is a space beyond the familiar structure of our thinking that we can access and that accessing it will transform all life as we know it.

What is beyond thought? Can we be still enough to find out? Devoted enough? Everything comes down to this!

The whole premise of *A Course in Miracles* is that yes, we can go beyond thought's limitations. Quite easily actually. It is very practical in this regard. It is very simple and clear: do this, then do that. We don't even have to believe in it. We just have to be willing. Read the text, do the lessons. The smallest beginning will lift us all the way to Heaven.

Gradually, as we practice, the belief system of separation is replaced by Oneness. This is in the nature of a return, a sudden awareness of what was given to us by God, and how that gift remains pure and whole and true right here, right now. Everything becomes pristine and silent, like a smooth icicle in pure sunlight. Thought is not there. And nothing is that isn't God.

But it ends as soon as thought enters and says: I want this experience to be mine! As soon as I remember "me" and try to clutch experience to the self - to possess it, own it, manipulate it - it ends.

Oneness is what is - the given - and separation is the thought that reaches in and tries to make what is whole and One into many fragments.

We can observe this movement in our thoughts if we are attentive. If we watch them - how they arise, what they do, where they go, what they ask of us, how we respond - we can see how they make time real and how they shift us away from being to becoming.

It feels very natural to us to be in time and to be devoted to becoming, to self-improvement, but as we begin to experience the alternative, we see that in fact it is separation and fragmentation that are deeply unnatural. The calm stillness of inner peace - lit by the Christ inherent in all of us - is our true natural state.

All this can seem very mystical and abstract, but it is not. We are living the separation right this very moment, and we can choose to live the alternative right now too.

When we do that, we see how thought is illusory - and how perception is illusory. We see how thin and wispy it is when compared to reality. And so naturally - and readily - we choose to return to God who is always waiting, always ready for us.

QUESTION: I like what you are saying but it also feels to me like not exactly what *A Course in Miracles* is saying. The course says that the world is not real, but you are actually talking about it as if it *is* real – that there is a past, that our brains evolved, that bodies are real . . .

ANSWER: It is real so long as we believe it is real and so we have to work out salvation within it. Otherwise we are just pretending that sleep is wakefulness and wakefulness is sleep. The only way out of illusion is to see it clearly for what it is and not resist it through judgment which always brings in time and effort. That is how illusions are undone.

I am not disputing that there is a state of oneness that falls outside time and space - and outside language, too - but I am saying, and I think the course is saying as well, that we don't just click our heels three times and go there. It takes work to recover that state. Otherwise we would be there now and there wouldn't be any need for the course or religion or whatever.

If you look at lesson 132 it says very clearly that the central idea *A Course in Miracles* aims to teach is that there is no world. But the course also says – and this is very important – that our readiness to learn that lesson means that it will be delivered to us in a form that we can both recognize and understand. The form of the lesson is going to vary – from tradition to tradition and even from person to person. So it's no good just quoting the course. We have to encounter it in the world, in these bodies. That's the only way we will learn in an experiential way - which is to say, the only way we will see - what is true and what is false.

Atonement dawns as slowly – maybe even slower – than separation. But it does dawn. In this world, in these bodies, it is possible to begin to catch glimpses of what awakening means and what it will feel like. It is possible to find the teachers who are going to lead us out of it. Jesus, *A Course in Miracles*, the Upanishads, Sri Aurobindo, psychotherapy. They are all just forms that appear in the world of illusion to teach us to distinguish the false from the true. That's all.

What I am saying is that we are moving in the direction of atonement and that atonement is in a sense evolving within us – just as separation did – so that we are going to perceive its manifestations outside of us well. We are going to begin to see the end of separation.

QUESTION: My body feels very real to me.

ANSWER: To your body, the material world is always going to be real. That is never going to be in dispute. Your toes, your friends, the ocean, the moon – all of it. But questioning materiality is actually not that interesting, if you think about it.

What is really interesting is the way we hate some people and love others. The way our minds incline to specialness - that is interesting. That is worth seeing and undoing. If you look at what it going on in your thoughts, and try to make contact with that hatred and anger and love . . . that is where the conflict is. That is where we are making enemies and going to war. And that is all our personal interpretation and opinion – it is all thought. And it is illusory because it has nothing to do with the fact – the person standing before us.

So our focus has to shift from the external to the internal and then we have to be in relationship with what we encounter there. What is thought doing? How is it behaving? Who is this self who seems to be observing and directing? Those are all important questions – and the more we look at them and engage with them, we are going to reach increasingly subtle realms of consciousness. We are going to begin to experience the holy place where thoughts cannot go, as the course puts it. We reach the mind that is the ground of being – this is not a personal experience but an impersonal one because it belongs to all of us equally. And as we get closer to it, and eventually reach it, we also begin to naturally help others move in its direction as well. Remember what the course says at the end of lesson 41: it is possible to reach God – it is the most natural thing in the world.

QUESTION: If we can reach God now then doesn't that mean the atonement is now, too, and not something that happens over millions of years?

ANSWER: We could look at it that way, but we also have to keep in mind that a critical idea in the course – in fact, what really sets it apart from a lot of other non-dual paths – is its emphasis on unity with our brothers and sisters. We do not enter the Kingdom alone, because the Kingdom is all of us. Now it's true that equality in eternity does not equal equality in time, so some of us – like Jesus or Tara Singh or Saint Therese or Emily Dickinson or whomever – come along and it seems like they've got it. They're enlightened awakened beings in contrast with our confused petty selves. But the thing is, if we aren't there with them, then they aren't there either. Heaven is all of us or it isn't Heaven. Period. The course suggests that some – once they are awakened – choose to stay here to help others. That is really a very beautiful idea. If we adopt the metaphor of Heaven as a place, then it's like we get all the way to its gates and and the gates open but we don't walk through because there's a whole line of people behind us and we don't want to go in because they can't go in with us. So we turn back in order to help them. That is a supremely loving gesture! It is very consistent with the Bodhisattva tradition in Buddhism – the delaying of personal enlightenment in order to help all sentient beings attain it. So we are working on ending separation at the personal level but it is helpful to remember that we are doing it collaboratively, that we are working together. Actually, there are many times when the course observes that our efforts are resounding in eternity and people we've never met physically and will never meet physically are being helped. Sometimes it is nice in the morning to give thanks to those nameless many whose prayerful lives are lifting us, even though we cannot see or touch them. And then also to remember that our own work in this regard is not just about us – not just about people that we love – but really about all of life. We are all in this together.

THE SAFETY OF GOD IS

We long for conclusion: that singular insight which will end our seeking, that knowledge which neither yields to nor gives rise to further questioning. It is certainty we crave, an antidote to the continual struggle within ourselves and against what is forever changing without. It is like we are caught in a flowing stream and all our effort is given to reaching an island on which to land, rest, and set up some shelter from which we might finally perceive the stream in its entirety, its wholeness.

But what if this impulse to go to ground - to settle in a vague attempt at permanence - is itself the impediment to certainty? In other words, what if we are the flow itself, and our desire for something perceptually stable – something static and contained - is what prevents us from the peace of knowing ourselves as we are in truth?

Is it possible we are flow? That observer and observed not separate but one fluid movement unto eternity?

One way to think about miracles in *A Course in Miracles* is that they relate the body to what is not of the body. Through the miracle, we are able to transcend the perceptual realm of the time-bound, matter-bound brain and make contact with - in order - stillness, eternity, and the all-encompassing reality of God's Mind. We move beyond what language can touch.

We are either extending wholeness or we are extending a belief system – political, religious, economic, ecological, psychological, spiritual or some amalgamation thereof - as a replacement, as a substitute, for wholeness. And if we are not careful, then we will neatly fold *A Course in Miracles* right into this. We will make it a belief system grounded in right and wrong. We can become subtly, almost unconsciously, loveless: I get it and you don't. So we have to be vigilant.

Often, when I experience myself in the presence of God - of that which goes nameless, of *what is* - it is only because I am still enough to briefly set aside the systemic prejudices and biases that are so characteristic of the human split mind, identification with which is literally what it means to be separated from God. Nothing dramatic happens when I am in this space other than that I surrender egoic notions of self and simply experience what remains. And what remains is love and it does not judge or condemn, not even a little.

So in those moments, I do not ask the pine

tree to be a symbol of beauty suitable for a poem, and I do not ask the pond to be a lake, and I do not demand the brook's slow trickle resemble one of Chopin's nocturnes. And I know that what is happening is given to all of us and is not in any way a reflection on me personally. As soon as I try to make it about me - my experience, my insight, my wisdom - then it dissolves. We receive the gift *for* everyone and *with* everyone or we don't receive it all.

That is a critical lesson in our slow enfoldment back into God. We cannot clutch at what is always given, nor fall for the egoic lie that is given to us alone, as if Jesus played favorites, as if God perceived Creation not as an undivided whole but in fragments, some more desirable than others.

We glimpse perfection simply because we know - or remember, perhaps - that imperfection is just a consequence of seeing from the fragmented rather than the whole (or healed) mind. It is a consequence of accepting busy-ness instead of stillness. This is not complicated. It is simply a decision that we can make at any time but must remember to make. We are out of the habit of thinking with God. But that does not mean that God is gone.

We have to remember: stillness is not just the body at rest (though it may be that too) but something far deeper and grander than the body. Stillness is not a retreat from the world, nor the absence of the world's effects. Rather, it is a state in which the world and its effects are perceived rightly, which is to say that they are held as is - free of our need to alter or improve them - and so they go without effect. When we are not making demands of life, we are able to perceive life clearly and lovingly. This is all that healing is.

Really, so much of our anguish comes from simply wanting to change things, which is always a resistance to *what is*, and thus reflects our lack of faith in a loving God. Who truly places their trust in God by definition knows peace. Who does not yet know peace is still just trusting God in name only. We can intuit our faith in God by the measure of our desire that things be other than what they are.

In a sense then, to be still is to understand the true source of causation without either denying or projecting it. To be still is to accept that salvation is simple and that it both begins and ends within us. It is of us, because we are of God, in the same way that the river touching *this* bank is also the river touching *that* bank.

Any conclusion - any perceived (or conceivable) end - reflects a linearity that is not of God. There is no end to *what is* as there is no beginning: there is merely the continual flow. It is not even circular; it cannot be contained or explained by geometry or anything else circumscribed by language. That is why *A Course in Miracles* (in concert with so many other traditions considering the Absolute) refuses to define God.

> We say 'God is,' and then we cease to speak, for in that knowledge words are meaningless. There are no lips to speak them, and no part of mind sufficiently distinct to feel that it is now aware of something not itself. It has united with

its Source. And like its Source Itself, it merely is.

I am not suggesting that those moments when I most clearly and lucidly know that "[o]neness is simply the idea God is" are an end, or even a stage presaging some further development. They are glimpses of the truth continually given, temporarily perceived in form but hardly limited thereby. It calls us because it is what sustains us: the always-given, always-giving. They reflect the truth that the world is nothing more than a series of chances "to perceive another situation where God's gift can once again be recognized as ours!"

In order to experience this - to bring it into application - we have to bring a sense of order into our lives, which means that we have to undo our sense of a personal life full of personal external activities, all of which demand our attention and distract us from God. The only way that we can end projection - which is also the end of seeking and the cyclical nature of binge and unfulfillment - is to bring the personal activity of thought to silence and stillness.

It is a decision - a choice we make - to seek the continually-extending grace of God and to locate ourselves within it. It is the opposite of personality. It is neither an end nor a conclusion; nor is it a beginning. It is rather a recognition that we are *what is*, outside perception and beyond concepts. The course describes this in its last chapter when it teaches that "[a]ll creation recognizes You, and knows You as the only Sources it has. Clear in Your likeness does the light shine forth from everything that lives and moves in You."

QUESTION: When you say stillness, I think of meditation.

ANSWER: Meditation can be a form of stillness. It can certainly facilitate an awareness of stillness. Nothing in *A Course in Miracles* says don't meditate in a formal way, but nothing says that we have to either. What we want to be sensitive to is the conviction that this form of meditation is more right than another, or that meditation generally is more right than some other expression of stillness. When that happens we are no longer in the presence of stillness. We have fallen back into the systemic thinking that is a disturbance of stillness, because it is an avoidance of stillness. We are back in the conceptual world of right and wrong out of which only conflict can arise.

For me, meditation is about walking outside, often before or just after dawn. There is a kind of attentiveness in those moments that is vastly healing, whether I am looking at apple blossoms or deer tracks or the reflection of the moon in a puddle. But that is just me. We all have our own mode, our own form. What matters is not getting so invested in a particular form that we overlook the content to which it directs us.

In general, when we find ourselves thinking in terms of right or wrong, or when we want everybody to be doing things the way we are, then we are not making contact with stillness. Once you make contact with stillness, you really see how the form is just utilitarian. It's like receiving a letter from someone you love. You're grateful for the envelope - it did its thing - but it is the letter that you are focused on.

QUESTION: Finding the form that represents that stillness is hard. I find that I tend to want what other people have – your forest, somebody's monastery, somebody else's retreat.

ANSWER: We are always projecting our holiness. And we are always evading our responsibility for bringing projection to an end. So-and-so has a better prayer practice, or a more authentic spiritual life, or has discovered the secret to untold health and riches, or whatever. We all do it.

We have to do some investigating when this happens. When I am fixated on somebody this way I have to ask: am I really being called to what this person symbolizes? Or I am just avoiding my own unique call? God is always speaking to us. And what is external is always helpful in discerning what God is saying. Sometimes it is in the nature of being reminded, okay, this is not my thing, I'm just falling in love with the ideal I think this person or practice represents. Other times, there really is something there to look into.

So you know, we try it out. I have a lot of friends - people I admire - who are into the law of attraction. They read the books, listen to the CDs, go to conferences. So I looked into it. Over a period of a year or so I gave some attention to it. Read the books, talked to people, listened to some classes, tried to do some of what was suggested. And it just didn't click. I'm glad I looked at it - that is the nature of openness and willingness, it will investigate and not be afraid of what it discovers - but it wasn't for me. And as a consequence, my practice of *A Course in Miracles* was strengthened. I was less distracted from it. I had some more conviction that for me it was the most helpful form.

So we never know. We feel these impulses and we have to just gently look into them and see what happens. There are no hard and fast rules, right? Basically we want to be kind and loving and let the spiritual chips fall where they may.

BECOMING FOOLISH

Either we are a part of God's plan for salvation or we are practicing our own plan. We can't have it both ways - a little bit of God's plan and a little bit of ours. Or God's plan mostly but with a little flavor of our own tossed in like salt. *A Course in Miracles* is very clear: there is no middle ground in salvation. That can seem intimidating at first, but if we give it some space, we will discover the peace inherent in it. It allows for a helpful choice, a real decision.

> Reason will tell you that there is no middle ground where you can pause uncertainly, waiting to choose between the joy of Heaven and the misery of hell. Until you choose Heaven, you *are* in hell and misery.

What is God's plan for salvation? Rigorous honesty is necessary to answer that question because for most of us, the answer is that we really don't know what God's plan is. We can find a quote from the course or some other tradition or some guru or teacher. Wordiness abounds. We can forever substitute somebody else's idea about God's plan for the vacuum in our own minds. But if we are willing to look at our experience and really sit with it and not project our responsibility for awakening onto someone else, then we will admit that God's plan is a mystery to us. We will see that we are far too wrapped up in our own plans to give more than a passing glance at God's. Of course we don't want to say that. Who does? But it's true. Sooner or later we are going to have to admit this.

Getting clear on our willful ignorance is very helpful. When I am clear that I am more interested in me and my plans than in God and God's Plan, I can give some close attention to my own plan and how it is working. This matters! If I am going to deviate from God, at least I can study the effects of doing so. At least I can say if it is working or not. Maybe I have discovered something. The whole point of inquiry is that we never know but can find out.

When I look at my plan, I see that it is always centered on bodies - mostly my own, but I'm not opposed to using yours if it furthers my own goals. My plan is always centered on getting something that I believe will help me survive, that will help me avoid looking at the fear and guilt I feel as a result of having chosen to believe in separation from God. My plan is only concerned with others to the extent they serve my own wants and desires.

When you get down to it, my plan is to survive as long as possible in a world that is bent on making me suffer before it kills me. I can be sophisticated in hiding this, make it quite polished and subtle. It really isn't a very spiritual way to live, and I very much want to appear spiritual and sincere. So I'll dress it up on the surface. But sooner or later, I have to come to the question: what good is my plan for survival? What is surviving and what is it surviving? Is it making me happy? Is it bringing me peace? Does it allow me to serve my brothers and sisters?

These are good questions! We don't even have to answer them – we just have to raise them. That is because the ego's plan for salvation – our plan – is sustained by our refusal to look at it. Refusal to see is simply resistance and resistance is always painful. It is always this big effort with no good return. Part of the reason we're so unhappy and fearful is our insistence that we're not unhappy (denial) or, in the alternative, that the cause of our unhappiness isn't internal but out there somewhere (projection).

Either way, in order to get some relief, we have to raise our inclination towards hell and misery into the light of understanding. We have to look at denial and projection. We have to give attention to what we are doing – it is our decision to do this, and it is our responsibility. It cannot be done for us.

We are pulled in the direction of spiritual and religious life because we are unhappy and in conflict. We are broken and - however dimly - we recall a state of wholeness. Seeing this - accepting it as a premise - can we then ask how our plan for restoration to God's grace and the peace of Heaven is working and not resist the answer?

It is that clarity to which we are called by *A Course in Miracles*. That is the hinge upon which awakening always turns.

It is not a matter of concluding that we happier today than we were ten years ago or that we have become more patient or can quote more bible passages more fluidly or write more insightful poetry. All of that is simply improvement, amendments to the external self, the projected self. They aren't crimes against God and life, but they also don't reveal God and life to us. Rather, they function as a sort of unholy middle ground - a little getting better, a little staying the same - that keeps the reality of Heaven obscure. We cherish the so-called middle ground because it allows us to account for *some* progress while still holding onto the guilt and fear so necessary to the ego's survival. In the end, that is *our* plan for salvation: Heaven by degrees and always with the reservation that if we want to turn back, we can.

And in a way, our plan is quite successful. It does exactly what it's supposed to do. It allows for illusions of progress without ever really addressing the true source of our perceived separation from God. It never solves the problem but it is quite ingenious at rearranging the symptoms. And that is why we're still unhappy. That is why we are not at peace. We are a mess within and the world is a mess, too. On and on it goes.

And then one day - more exhausted than inspired - we just give it up. We fall to the side of the road and say, "I quit. I don't know what God's plan is but I know mine is not working. So I'm done. It's over." There is nothing admirable about it but that doesn't mean it's not a good moment. It is! It's the beginning of healing.

When we put our plan down - fully and finally - then God's plan is instantly revealed. Before that moment, the impulse is to pretend we already know God's plan. Or to say that yes, our plan is not working but only pretend to give it up. Or find some new method or system that this time - this time! - will allow us at last to tweak our own plan to perfection.

None of that will work. We have to let our plan go entirely. When we do, it is simply replaced by God's Plan because God's Plan is given; it is always there. But we will not know this until we have given up our plan entirely. Why? Because *there is no middle ground*. So we have to resist the impulse to pick anything else up – a new plan, a revised plan, a fragment of the old plan. Our job is to let go, not replace.

A Course in Miracles is very helpful at getting us to that place where we see the hollowness of our learning and the futility of the action that flows from it. That's really all it wants to teach us. It just wants to get us to that place where we can let go of our plan and make space for God's. That is the meaning of:

> The course does not aim at teaching the meaning of love, for that is beyond what can be taught. It does aim, however, at

removing the blocks to the awareness of love's presence, which is your natural inheritance.

We think we are students of the course in order to build magnificent temples. Really, we are students in order to learn that a) we wouldn't know magnificent if it wooed us with roses and chocolate and b) the temple - magnificent or otherwise - is already built.

The upheaval that attends letting go of our plan can be distressing. We often experience this undoing as unsettling and it can be painful indeed. But deeper than all that is the mighty sense of relief it affords. Some space emerges in which one can perceive at last the truth of "I need do nothing." One can be simply grateful for what is without feeling any need to rush in and embroider it with their own pattern, their own ideas.

I went a long time - lifetimes perhaps - trying to be wise. What a joy at last to be a fool, tripping happily through an enlightening dream, singing alleluia as I go.

HOW SIMPLE THE SOLUTION IS

There is a great story in the Zen tradition that you probably know. A farmer's horse runs away leaving him with no means to work the fields. "What a pity," his neighbors say. "Poor you."

"We'll see," says the farmer.

The next day the horse comes home leading three wild horses. "That's great!" say the neighbors. "Now you have four horses. Lucky you!"

"We'll see," says the farmer. "Maybe it's good, maybe it's not."

One thing to see about this farmer – because he is very wise – is that you can't push him to conclusions. He is not trying to please anyone by sharing their assumptions. It is a remarkable thing, really. He is just letting things be what they are – he doesn't even need to interpret them, much less change them. It is the wisdom of non-interference.

The next day the farmer's son tries to work one of the new horses. He wants to break it in to farm work. But it throws the young man hard and his leg breaks. "Wow," say the neighbors. "That's really too bad."

And you know what the farmer says, right? He says, "maybe it's bad. Maybe it's good. We'll see."

The next day the army comes through, drafting able-bodied youths for war. Obviously they can't take the farmer's son. His injured leg allows him to avoid conscription. "Incredible news!" the neighbors say.

And the farmer - who is obviously a very patient man - says, "maybe it's good. Maybe it's bad."

And on and on it goes.

Most teaching around that story has to do with perception and refusing to draw conclusions based on perception. We really don't know what is going on and so it is pointless to settle on this or that preferred narrative. It is all just interpretation. That is what we really have to deal with – and what the farmer deals with so splendidly: undoing our inclination to conclude, to invest in interpretation as reality.

I am not the farmer in that story! I wish I was but I am not. I am the neighbor. I am the one who every days tells the farmer what's good and what's bad. I have an opinion about everything and I am always sharing it. And after I share it I go to the diner and talk about Heraclitus and *A Course in Miracles* and stillness and prayer with anybody who will listen – actually, it really doesn't matter who listens. And then I go home and share my opinions with my family. I'm so busy being wise and making sure everybody knows that I'm wise that the truth - and the faith that makes seeing truth possible - are lost to me. The truth is there – it doesn't go anywhere just because we're not giving attention to it – but I am too busy and chatty to perceive it.

Our intellectual busy-ness – the talking, the bustling, the thinking - can obscure the simple clarity that we remain as God created us. It impedes our capacity for vision. This is a fact – not an insight – and if we can relax our incessant self-promotion, then we will know it. There is nothing complicated or mystical about it. You let go of what is false and what is true is there. But we don't do it. We refuse. Why?

For a long time in my life, I had a particular experience with all of this. I would let go of what was false for a minute or two and perceive the still grace of God and then . . . I would take seriously the idea that "I" had done something serious and important to attain this grace. I would conclude that God's grace was a consequence of merit and effort – *my* merit and effort. And you see, as soon as I reach that conclusion then I am back in the perception of separation from God. Why? Because the perception of separate selves with separate interests and experience *is* the separation.

A Course in Miracles puts it this way:

> You are still convinced that your understanding is a powerful contribution to the truth, and makes it what it is. Yet we have emphasized that you need under-

stand nothing. Salvation is easy just *because* it asks nothing you cannot give right now.

I tend to skip over that last sentence because its implications are so powerful. *Salvation is easy just because it asks nothing you cannot give right now.* The whole course is contained in it. Whatever salvation requires is already literally at hand. I don't have to do another lesson of *A Course in Miracles*, re-read Tara Singh, meditate more or wake up at 4 a.m. and walk the dog through snowy woods while muttering prayers to Jesus. Those are the rituals the egoic self offers in place of the simple truth that if I'd like to wake up - right now - then I can.

So if I am willing to really read that sentence - if I am willing to give it some space - then I am going to see that the reason I am not saved yet is because I don't want to be. I'm not ready. I am still deeply, even cunningly, resistant to love. And while that doesn't make Jesus pound whiskey in a backwoods roadhouse, it also doesn't leave me especially happy or peaceful. And I really want to be happy and peaceful. I really want to end conflict and come to the peace that surpasses understanding. But I am at war with myself over it – part of me wanting to let go and part holding on like a dog.

What do I do?

More and more it doesn't seem especially complicated. When I am unhappy and in conflict it is because I am keeping Jesus - that loving symbol of the healed mind - at a distance. Since that's the problem, the solution is to invite him back.

When I don't walk my dog, I get irritated. And it's funny in a way. Sometimes I'll be talking to Chrisoula, telling her that I didn't walk the dog yesterday and here it is 9 a.m. and I still haven't walked the dog and why do I do this to myself? And to the dog? Why is life so full and busy that I forget about my loyal dog? Is it because I hate God? Or God hates me? Does God hate dogs? Why do I love being separated from truth so much? Maybe I should read some more Augustine or Krishnamurti. Maybe I should write a blog post about all this. Or maybe I should return to the Catholic church and go to confession.

And Chrisoula will say gently, "why don't you take the dog for a walk right now?"

I forget how simple the solution is! I like talking and thinking! The first time I sat in a Zendo, the teacher said that we were going to practice not paying attention to our thoughts and I thought to myself, "you must have some really boring thoughts." There was no way I was going to let go of that egoic voice – it was smart, eloquent, charming, funny, creative. I felt bad for people whose thoughts were so simple and bland they could actually let go of them.

She was right though, of course. The truth needs nothing at all from us. And that is not an insult. It is our freedom. And it is ours whenever we are ready.

QUESTION: Are you saying that we have to take action through our bodies in order to feel peaceful? Like walking your dog or going to a Zendo?

ANSWER: In a way, yes. But if we look at that process closely, the body is actually more of a neutral participant. If we are attentive to what is happening internally, we may learn at some point that we are really not serious about waking up or about the relationships that help us to wake up. When we see that clearly, we can also see that the result of that casualness, that lack of seriousness, is some form of conflict – it hurts. It brings sadness and pain and grief. And a time comes when that is no longer tolerable and so we decide to do something: we decide to see if there is another way, a better way, as Bill Thetford so helpfully said to Helen Schucman. I have always loved that story - the course literally comes into existence because one person wants to find a way to live without conflict and somebody else - who is intimated in that conflict - agrees to help him find it. That is *A Course in Miracles*!

So all of that - that realization of pain, the unwillingness to put up with it - is an internal process. It happens at the level of mind, very much irrespective of what we are doing with our bodies. However, when we reach that space, it is actually liberating and so our external experience begins to mirror it. It begins to reflect that liberation, that nod in the direction of peace and joy. So in the example I gave about walking the dog, this openness is reflected in my willingness to hear Chrisoula offer me some very sound advice, and my willingness too to go ahead and act on it it. That happens a lot – somebody else will give us a little nudge, often no more than a casual suggestion – and it is exactly what we need and so we follow it. The real movement there is internal – the willingness, the openness. It is "having the ears to hear," in a way.

There will always be an external expression of our internal decision to align our thinking with Christ. Often these will occur so close in time that it is almost impossible to distinguish them in terms of cause and effect. But if we are really attentive to the subtle action of mind and its relation to what it is outside, we will see that the internal precedes the external.

QUESTION: Isn't there a danger though of becoming attached to the external form or expression or whatever you call it? Why bother with the external at all? Why not just focus on the internal?

ANSWER: That is certainly a risk. We can become attached to anything – even to the idea of being attached! That is what the ego does – what a split mind does – it seizes on something and says "mine!" and then defends it. So we have to be vigilant, and we have to ask for help in undoing that. Well, most of us do. I certainly do.

In terms of why bother with what is external, I think the only reason to do so is that we think it's real, and so in effect it *is* real. I can say that my dog is an illusion, and I might be metaphysically correct (at least from the perspective of *A Course in Miracles*), but is that really helpful? Faking spiritual insight by repeating ideas I've memorized is truly unhelpful in the sense that it blocks knowledge almost entirely. So long as we believe the body is real – and we all do believe that for the most part – it is best to use it in as gentle and kind a way as possible. Hold the metaphysics loosely and love to the greatest degree you can manage. Allow the expression of God its movement. Just let it flow through the body without giving it a lot of thought, without trying to control it. Trust that if your mind is in accord with God's – if it is even just *willing* to be in accord with God's – then the external manifestation will be precisely what you and everybody else needs at that particular time.

It's a fine line, I know. And it can be very confusing. But if we are attentive to what is going on internally – if we really make that the focus of our energy and practice – then the external will become a helpful mirror. The interior and exterior landscapes are not so separate from one another in the ultimate sense. When we're ready to let it go altogether, we'll know. Until that time it's like Saint Augustine said: "love and do what you will."

THE INFINITE PATIENCE OF THE HOLY SPIRIT

One of the more challenging concepts we find in *A Course in Miracles* is that we are not bodies. The course does not mean this is a compromised way - that we are souls temporarily residing in physical bodies. It does not mean it metaphorically. It means literally that what we are in truth has nothing to do with what is external, the body.

> When you equate yourself with a body you will always experience depression. When a child of God thinks of himself in this way he is belittling himself, and seeing his brothers as similarly belittled.

The Holy Spirit – which is our healed mind, that part of the mind which does not acknowledge itself as separated from God - does not share this egoic and material view of the body. It sees it the same way it sees trees and turtles and coconut cream pies: a means of communication through which a sick and fragmented mind can be healed and made whole. This is the whole value of the world - when shared with the Holy Spirit, it becomes a means of atonement. The separation cannot prevail when we surrender judgment to the one who knows better.

> The Holy Spirit does not see the body as you do, because He knows the only reality of anything is the service it renders God on behalf of the function He gives it.

If we want to know which teacher we are working with - the ego or the Holy Spirit – then all we have to do is check in with our perception of our brothers and sisters. Not the ones that we love readily, but the ones that we hate, secretly or otherwise. Take an inventory. Can you call to mind one person, the mere memory of whom brings to your mind anger or hate or guilt or depression or fear? Answer yes and you know that no matter how peaceful or happy you appear to be, you are still not committed to Jesus and the Holy Spirit. You are still holding onto some shred of your own plan for salvation.

It's important not to berate ourselves for this. So you are filled with anger and hatred for a fellow human being - so what? Very few of us - very very few of us - are entirely free of that. Indeed, holiness resides not in having no anger or hatred but rather in *seeing* that anger and hatred clearly, which is to say, without judgment, without rushing to do something to do it. Only when we reach this clarity, this willingness to face what is broken and ugly can it begin to be healed.

> [a]ll loss comes only from your own misunderstanding. Loss of any kind is impossible. But when you look upon a brother as a physical entity, his power and glory are "lost" to you and so are yours. You have attacked him, but you must have attacked yourself first. Do not see him this way for your own salvation, which must bring him his.

This is why kindness – which in the text and workbook is never explicitly taught as part of our practice of *A Course in Miracles* - is actually very important to the course's useful application. In general, we don't heal first and then start looking for Christ in one another. We have to seek Christ out - and even bring Christ out – in our brothers and sisters before we feel its effects. There is a certain "act as if" principle at play. We might not know how to perceive salvation in one another, but we can do a lot of good by approaching each other in the spirit of salvation. If I am willing to see Christ in you, then Christ will be revealed to both of us. And the same is true for you - if you will perceive Christ in me, we will together see Christ. Our contribution is always the willingness. The rest will follow. It is a law and we can rely upon it totally. But our willingness is precedent.

When we treat our brothers and sisters as if they are the key to salvation, then we tend to promote a spirit of peace and fellowship in which even more learning and healing is facilitated.

That is right use of the body. And its fruits are for everyone - including ourselves.

> Guided by the Holy Spirit . . . [the body] becomes a means by which the part of the mind you tried to separate *from* spirit can reach beyond its distortions and return to spirit. The ego's temple thus becomes the temple of the Holy Spirit, where devotion to Him replaces devotion to the ego.

In a way, this is why the metaphysics of the course can be a distraction. It's good to know them and to have them on hand, but not if they keep us entangled in intellectual navel-gazing. Whether we want to admit it or not, we believe that we're here in the world, having all these experiences of the body. Why not - with the assistance of the Holy Spirit - devote those experiences to enlightening our dim understanding of God? Even just a little? As the course points out "[H]ealing is the result of using the body solely for communication."

> Mind cannot be made physical, but it can be made manifest *through* the physical if it uses the body to go beyond itself. By reaching out, the mind extends itself. It does not stop at the body . . .

Thus, the only use to which the Holy Spirit will put the body is to communication. That is the only use to which we should put it as well. Really, it is the only helpful use to which we *can* put it. This takes time to learn, but our willingness to try - to fumble along, to not hide our ineptitude - is never without reward. The way to joy and peace is through the illusion we have made - our bodies, other bodies, the world with its trees and turtles and delicious desserts and political strife and so on and so forth.

As we practice heeding the Holy Spirit's singular purpose, we begin to experience the promise of God's love. And if we fall short? If we find ourselves hating a neighbor because their dog barks too loud? Or a certain teacher because they gave us a low grade? Or on this or that politician because they are so heartless and greedy and ignorant?

It's okay. It is impossible for us to make mistakes that the Holy Spirit cannot fix. That is what the Holy Spirit is for. Our errors are without effect which is why the course can say they therefore never happened.

> The power of wholeness is extension. Do
> not arrest your thought in this world,
> and you will open your mind to creation
> in God.

We don't really need to make special time for the Holy Spirit. We don't need to be in a church or on a zafu and we don't need any special training or certification. Rather, we simply need to give attention to the two ways of seeing: do we perceive our brothers and sisters as bodies? Or as the very light and love of salvation itself? All salvation – the promise of inner peace itself – hinges on our decision to see one way or the other. Nor is there any middle ground.

If we are honest, then we will probably admit that we *want* to see our brothers and sisters as light and love but in truth are perceiving them more in terms of bodies. Again, that is not a crisis. When we see that we are falling short of seeing as Christ sees, of seeing as the Holy Spirit would have us see, then we can ask for assistance. We can change our mind in favor of another way. Help is always given – that is the nature of the Holy Spirit and its infinite patience. We are always blessed when we avail ourselves of the blessing of the one who knows what blessing is and what it is for.

THE GIVEN

    I often talk about of God - or awakening - in terms of an internal recognition or realization of "the given." What I mean by that is simply that God is here. God is here now. God's grace and love are present to you - *are* you - in a very real and knowable way. We merely accept the gift - the Treasure of God - that was extended in creation. There is nothing else to do. There is nothing else we *can* do.

> There is no question but one you should ever ask of yourself; - "Do I want to know my Father's Will for me?" He will not hide it. He has revealed it to me because I asked it of Him, and learned of what He had already given.

One or Two Steps Only

It is tempting to complicate this - to analyze it, cross-reference it to other sections of the text or certain lessons in the workbook. Maybe bring in other spiritual traditions. We can meditate on the ancient story of the prodigal son (to which the course makes reference), gleaning perhaps some sense of the intensity and unconditional nature of God's love for Creation. Perhaps this is unavoidable. But we are not called to master the text in an intellectual way. We are called to the spirit that informs the text, and thereby to make it a reality in our lives. We are here to bring the course into application.

And how do we do that? In a sense, we act it out. The prodigal son wastes his gifts, disrespects his father, suffers in exile and finally crawls back in shame. What does the father do in response? He celebrates the return of his beloved. Without our creations - without love - we are not whole. Can we see our brothers and sisters as prodigals? Can we welcome them that way? Can we allow them to do the same for us? I mean this literally: can we love our brothers and sisters without qualification?

> God wants only His Son because His Son is His only treasure. You want your creations as He wants His . . . Your function is to add to God's treasure by creating yours. His Will *to* you is His Will *for* you. He would not withhold creation from you because His joy is in it. You cannot find joy except as God does.

This business of loving one another as God loves us . . . it can drive us crazy if we try to make sense of it in worldly terms. The world does not know this love – it does not respect this love. It gives no space to this love. We are not talking about romance here. We are not talking about one body to another. We are talking about something so much more than that. We really have to surrender the world's standard. We have to let it go. As the course teaches, "[Y]ou cannot behold the world and know God." By the terms of the world, the prodigal got what was coming to him. Justice demands no less.

But the justice of God hews to a different standard. It asks us to accept a love that appears reckless and even dangerous. Love the way God loves and the world will write you off as a fool or worse. Jesus was not executed for nothing. But only that radical love – only that love that the world calls dangerous – will truly satisfy us. If we are honest, we will see that we merit no less.

> Your heart lies where your treasure is, as His does. You who are beloved of God are wholly blessed. Learn this of me, and free the holy will of all those who are as blessed as you are.

We take our lead from Jesus who learned that the given - God's love - was indistinguishable from his (as it is from our) brothers and sisters. Together we are God's joy. Together we are Creation. When we accept this, we naturally extend it to one another. It won't make any sense in terms of the world. But in a deeper way, it will be more natural and easy than breathing itself. We are saved by Love *for* Love. And being so saved, we naturally save each other.

QUESTION: But what if that is not my experience? What if I just don't know myself that way?

ANSWER: Actually, it is not really critical that we know ourselves that way. What is critical is that we trust that God knows us that way. That is what the story of the prodigal son models for us: the unconditional love of God for all Creation, without exception, regardless of what we are doing with respect to that love. The course is saying – as in some ways Christianity has been saying for two thousand years – that you and God are one in a very real and tangible way. Separation is not possible. In ACIM terms, the prodigal only dreamed he was far away and suffering in hair shirts, eating roots with pigs or whatever. He was always beloved of God, so he was always home.

If it was a matter of finding ways to love ourselves on our own we would probably be doomed. So we don't really bother with that. Instead, we try to make contact with the healed part of our mind, the part of it that remembers its unbreakable union with God, and we nurture relationship with that part. We give attention to it. In the beginning, we have to take on faith that those efforts are going to be met and honored. We have to trust that God is not going to say no to us. But we do have to show up. The prodigal only learns he is forgiven when he returns. So God will do the heavy lifting; our job is simply to show up and ask that it be done.

QUESTION: It sounds simple when you say it that way. But it never stays that way in my head. In a few minutes or an hour or next week it's all going to be complicated and difficult again.

ANSWER: Yes. That happens to all of us. That is how it goes for those who are still learning! *A Course in Miracles* is a process: we grow over time. That is how it happens. There is a moment and a place in which time and space and our evolution within them disappear, but until that happens, we are simply flawed and fallen beings learning to remember wholeness. So yes – it is simple and sometimes we see that, and can act on it, and then it becomes complex again. We remember spirit in this moment and in the next we forget about spirit altogether. That's how it goes.

I appreciate the frustration inherent in that, by the way. What helps me not fall into bitterness or anger is to remember a couple of things. The first is that as I practice, I get better. The more I remember God's grace, the more grace remains with me when my mind wanders. So periods of fear and anger and conflict become less intense and their duration shortens. This motivates me to keep at it and not give up. Sometimes that is all we need – a reminder that we're doing great and that our efforts are yielding results.

And second, I remember – in an idealistic kind of way – that the end is sure because none of this really happened. That is a crazy concept to appreciate in worldly terms, but I don't really have to understand it in order to make use of it. I can take it on faith. God has not left me bereft – the progress I alluded to before is proof of this – and so I am going to work on the assumption that God never ever will give up on me. Part of working *A Course in Miracles* has to do with being confident that it works and is not full of nonsense, is not just a bunch of pretty spiritual poetry going nowhere. I may not have experienced the coming true of all its promises – and some of its concepts may prove harder to accept and practice than others – but I am manifesting confidence that it will work no matter what.

In the text, there is a lovely passage that assures us that we never left God, that we have done everything right, that we are loving one another perfectly, and that Creation is humming along in eternity just fine. So I say okay. Maybe today that seems like a pipe dream but okay. I am going to hold onto that like a light to see me through these darker and harder places.

QUESTION: Part of me sometimes feels like needing that light is a sign of failure – like it makes me weak. If I was better at this, then I would just be able to do it.

ANSWER: We all hate crutches. That's pride talking and it talks in all of us and we all listen. But the thing is, you aren't alone. The ego says that we're failures – that we're weak and infirm. Behind those accusations is an even greater one: that God would be perfectly justified in shunning us, in leaving us outside the gates of Heaven. It's like the egoic self wants to do some spiritual culling – thinning the herd of its weakest links. So when we recognize our need for help, the first judgment we lay on it is that God is going to kill us *because* we need that help. So naturally we are resistant to lights and crutches and floatation devices or whatever metaphor works best for us.

But here's the thing – here's what the ego never reveals to us. *We aren't the only ones who need help.* Everybody does. *Everybody*. We all need some form of help. Some students need a teacher who is physically present to them on the phone, online and in workshops. Some of us – I am an example of this – need to read a lot about the course, over and over – in order to feel okay, to feel safe. Others need the comfort of study groups. Some of us need to pray all the time, or do yoga, or write spiritual poems or paint icons or whatever. Who cares? Everybody who opens *A Course in Miracles* is doing it because they need help and – on some level – are ready to accept it.

So we have to avoid those inclinations to beat ourselves up. And one way to do that is to remember how much others need us to do this work. *I* need you to do it. We are doing this work together. It's not just about us.

ON MISTAKES AND FORGIVENESS

Like all students of *A Course in Miracles* I make mistakes. I get frustrated with people. I can be very impatient and patronizing. I'm greedy sometimes - for food, for attention, for praise. I allow myself to be casual and lazy in my spiritual practice. I skip walking the dog because it's raining or I'm tired or I'm in a bad mood. You know how it goes. We all do it and we all wish we didn't.

A Course in Miracles teaches us both why we make these errors, how to correct them and - ultimately and most importantly - how to get to a place where there *is* no such thing as error. In a way, we are learning through the course to be kinder, gentler and wiser people - true examples of radical healing - here in the world while simultaneously learning that it's all in the nature of a dream and healing really isn't necessary at all.

Our errors - regardless of their seeming magnitude and effect - are all a result of confusion about what we are in truth and what our role is in God's plan for salvation.

> The plan is not yours because of your
> limited ideas about what you are. This
> sense of limitation is where all errors
> arise. The way to undo them, therefore, is
> not *of* you but *for* you.

When we believe that we are bodies - perhaps with souls attached and perhaps not - then we are going to try and defend those bodies. We are going to identify with their appetites and desires and insecurities. We are going to look at our brothers and sisters as if they're bodies too - sometimes pleasing us, sometimes hurting us - but always with separate and competing interests. It is a recipe for destructiveness. It is a situation premised on – and devoted to sustaining – a deep sense of loss. Once we make this error, there is no way to fix it from within its effects.

That is why forgiveness in *A Course in Miracles* constantly urges us to overlook error and to see one another not as bodies engaged in a frantic dance of scarcity and suffering but as equal thoughts in the Mind of God forever bent on remembering that Holy and unified state.

> Look, then, beyond error and do not let
> your perception rest upon it, for you will
> believe what your perception holds. Ac-

cept as true only what your brother is, if you would know yourself.

Of course, if it were that easy, then we'd already have done it and there wouldn't be any need for *A Course in Miracles* or any other spiritual path or tradition. And the course acknowledges as much: "You do not understand how to overlook errors, or you would not make them." So what do we do? How do we ensure that our perception will not rest on error but rather see beyond it to the Love that is our singular reality?

Central to the practice of *A Course in Miracles* is our willingness to accept a new guide or teacher in place of our egoic selves. Seeing the uselessness of our own teaching efforts, we effectively resign and ask the Holy Spirit (or Jesus, if that is more a comfortable model) to make decisions for us.

> Forgiveness through the Holy Spirit lies simply in looking beyond error from the beginning, and thus keeping it unreal for you. Do not let any belief in its realness enter your mind, or you will also believe that you must undo what you have made in order to be forgiven. What has no effect does not exist, and to the Holy Spirit the effects of error are non existent. By steadily and consistently canceling out all its effects, everywhere and in all respects, He teaches that the ego does not exist and proves it.

Practically speaking, this means that we have to turn to the Holy Spirit. We have to remind ourselves every five minutes - every minute if that's what it takes - that we need help and that help is here if we are ready to accept it. Talk to the Holy Spirit. Get on your knees and ask to be guided. Read a few lines of the course whenever you can so that it is fresh. When we become students of *A Course in Miracles*, we become followers, not leaders, and Life itself depends on our remembering the distinction.

Sustained effort in this regard is never without results. The form of asking for help doesn't matter so long as the content - the need itself - is not being hidden or otherwise evaded. We slow down and a sense of calmness enters. Even if we're scared and uncertain, we can perhaps make contact with the willingness that there is a better way, and that we are going to find it one way or the other, sooner or later.

As we begin to see the effects of looking at our lives with Jesus and the Holy Spirit, we become more confident that this kind of looking actually works. We aren't being led down a primrose path that only goes in circles. We aren't being sold a bill of spiritual goods. And we begin to see that forgiveness is natural - that we can extend Love to one another without worrying about the apparent external details. We start to practice forgiveness all the time. We start to get good at it.

> The Atonement is a lesson in sharing, which is given you because *you have forgotten how to do it*. The Holy Spirit merely

reminds you of the natural use of your abilities. By reinterpreting the ability to attack into the ability to share, He translates what you have made into what God created.

This is the way out. This is the way to fully recall our Oneness with God. This is the means by which we remember that we are only journeying to the remembrance that no journey is necessary.

Thus we practice forgiveness. We start with what is in front of us - the spouse who won't make the bed, the son or daughter who talks back, the boss who won't listen to our concerns and questions. We give it all to the Holy Spirit. Why not? We don't pretend to be spiritual giants and we don't worry about how messy it all looks. We are not the judge anymore. Our internal Teacher is revealed and so become devoted followers. In this way, often quicker and with more ease than we expected, worry and fear end, and Love - which is our natural profession and our one true calling – is all that remains in their place.

QUESTION: What if I can't find the Holy Spirit? It feels so abstract to me.

ANSWER: There is nothing to find. It is already there. If you are not in contact with it – and you will know if you are or are not – then it is only because you are placing your will between your mind and the thoughts that you think with God. It is that simple. So when we are not in contact with the Holy Spirit, then we don't go searching out the Holy Spirit, we need to search out what is hindering the relationship. What am I thinking that God would not think? What am I not thinking that God *would* think? And in that inquiry – if I give real attention to it – the Holy Spirit is revealed in a very tangible and helpful way.

I am trying to say – without falling into cliché or abstraction – that the Holy Spirit, being a part of you, cannot meaningfully be separate from you. We can be in denial about that, we can be forgetful about it, but we can't change the fact of it. What the Holy Spirit is and what your mind is are totally inseparable. They are one. So when we are not feeling that connection, then it is a question of taking some action – some internal action – to reestablish our awareness. Looking closely at what is going on – our feelings, our ideas, our obsessions and so forth – is a great way to do that. You just sink into it in a spirit of inquiry and then you realize that the Holy Spirit is there with you. You really can't do this alone.

QUESTION: I am confused about the distinction between the Holy Spirit and Jesus.

ANSWER: The Holy Spirit is that part of our mind that remembers oneness and is also aware of our decision to forget oneness. As such, it is a bridge between the unreality we have made and the reality that is God's Creation. Jesus is more in the nature of a role model or a coach. He made contact – sustained contact – with the Holy Spirit and his attention and devotion to it allowed him to become the Christ. We can all become the Christ; he shows us how, by showing us how to make contact with the Holy Spirit as he did, and learning its lessons.

That is generally how *A Course in Miracles* sees it. But it is important not to get hung up on that or overly attached to it. If it is more helpful to you to pray to Jesus, to look at your interior landscape with Jesus, then you should do so without feeling like you are breaking any laws or violating any codes or something like that. It is a question of what works – it really is.

We are all moving to a space that transcends this need for symbols in the first place. But we aren't there yet. So it is good while we are still moved by those images and ideas to make use of them, according to how they resonate inside us. There is a point where Jesus invites us to think of him as literally holding our hand while we do the lessons. So you know, the course clearly contemplates that we will rely on these symbols. It expects that of us.

ON SEEING DIFFERENTLY

A great deal of our practice as students of *A Course in Miracles* resides in seeing differently - on *learning* to see differently. Awakening begins that way. This process usually begins with our physical eyes: our physical sight. The early lessons of the workbook direct our attention to the pedestrian, the ordinary: tables, chairs, pens, shadows.

We are explicitly taught in the first lesson that "[O]ne thing is like another as far as the application of the idea is concerned."

In the second, we are urged to "[R]emain as indiscriminate as possible in selecting subjects for [the lesson's] application, do not concentrate on anything in particular, and do not attempt to include everything you see in a given area.

And in the third we are reminded that "whatever you see becomes a proper subject for applying the idea [of the lesson].

A very clear foundation is being laid, a principle that underlies the whole premise of *A Course in Miracles*: nothing can be excluded. It doesn't matter if we are gazing at a lovely rose, a breathtaking sunset, a deer dying on the side of the road, or a car accident on the interstate. It is all equal. It is all the same.

Of course, we don't believe this, even if we profess to intellectually. Obviously, a rose is nicer than roadkill. Obviously we would rather eat a loaf of bread than a plate full of stones. It makes sense, right?

But the course is not so focused on the object of our seeing so much as on *how* we see. We are being asked to question a method of seeing, and to evaluate its effects, and on that basis to consider an alternative. We are being asked to consider "another way."

The salient quality of the world that we perceive - which is the material world, the world of our senses - is its mutability. It changes. It holds no single unalterable meaning. Thus, I can fall weeping at the sight of a pink rose and somebody else can pass it by without a thought. Your comfort food is chocolate and chocolate makes me nauseated. And so on.

That world and the judgment upon which it rests feels very natural to us, but peace is not possible in it because of this lack of a sure foundation. The Gospel of Matthew alludes to this, when Jesus teaches that a house built on solid rock will withstand anything while the one built on shifting sands will inevitably collapse. Foundations matter.

Our goal then - and the objective of the lessons - is to stabilize our erratic and fickle perception and make of it a sounder foundation. We do this by questioning its propensity to declare what it sees as true. If we are attentive, we will notice that we almost always accept without question whatever thought tell us. It sees a sunset and declares it is beautiful. It sees a chair and declares it is practical. But this is always the past talking: and when the past talks, our mind is closed.

The workbook lessons – especially the early ones - aim to teach us to question the process and commit to something different.

> When you say, "Above all else I want to see this table differently," you are making a commitment to withdraw your preconceived notions about the table, and open your mind to what it is, and what it is for. You are not defining it in past terms. You are asking what it is, rather than telling it what it is. You are not binding its meaning to your tiny experience of tables, nor are you limiting its purpose to your little personal thoughts.

In essence, we are saying, "okay. My way of seeing does not bring me peace. So I am going to try again. What am I looking at? What does it mean?"

And rather than rush in with an answer, we wait. That's hard, but we can do it. Even if we withhold egoic judgment for just a few seconds, it is healing. It only takes a moment for God to show us there is another way, a better way. And there is nothing spectacular or dramatic about it. A chair is as good as a temple for learning purposes. *A Course in Miracles* is not particular in that regard. Our learning goes with us everywhere.

> Right perception is necessary before God can communicate directly to His altars, which He established in His Sons. There He can communicate His certainty, and His knowledge will bring peace without question.

This is something we can practice all the time. That is the whole point. Nothing is excluded: every thing is sufficient unto the lessons God would teach us. All we have to do is be willing to give attention.

QUESTION: How do we withhold judgment though? I appreciate that it is a good idea but it seems that when it comes to practice then the ego is just going to rush in and judge.

ANSWER: Then we give attention to the ego rushing in! That's what is in that moment. What does that feel like? How does it happen? In the early stages of this process, all we can do is notice – and sometimes we are only going to catch faint glimpses. But then it will slow down a little and the nuances will be revealed to us. The ego's rushing about feels out of control but we start to see that a decision is being made that empowers it to do what it does, and we are the ones making that decision. That is a big insight!

All of this takes time. It takes patience, because we are giving attention to what resists attention because it can only survive in the absence of attention. This is not a spiritual path for the faint of heart. It requires tenacity and courage. It really does. It requires a certain work ethic. So you know, that is what we do: we show up and give attention to what is happening. And over time, more is revealed.

QUESTION: And when it is revealed it is undone?

ANSWER: Clear unequivocal seeing is undoing but again, it takes most of us time to get there. We aren't ready for it yet because to see that way is very scary and destabilizing. We have this whole thought system in place and everything from the orbit of the moon to the tides to what we eat for breakfast and who our favorite writer is is tied up in it. That is where the patience comes in. We could drop the whole ego charade in a second but most of us do it through a series of baby steps until one day without really giving it much thought we are free.

Remember that undoing is what the Holy Spirit does. That's its job. If it was up to us to undo we would get all confused and demanding. That is the point of seeing that our plan for salvation is unworkable. So undoing is sort of like something we put off to the side and don't worry about. If you go to the dentist to have your teeth cleaned, you just have to get yourself to the dentist. You don't have to actually do all the cleaning yourself. So it's like that. We are just showing up and giving attention and the heavy lifting is being done at another level by an intelligence that is in us but not of us.

A FOCUS ON HOW

As students of *A Course in Miracles* we are focused not on *what* we see but rather on *how* we see. This represents a radical shift in being and few of us make it painlessly or in one fell swoop. It takes time; it is a process. It is nice to know that we are learning together.

Walking out of the forest this morning, the dog tree'd two bear cubs. An owl watched as I circled the pond. The mergansers paddled cautiously away, hiding in thick cattail. The trail was pocked with deer tracks, some no larger than a quarter: fawns tottering after their mothers home.

We see all this: and we assign meaning to it. First we name it. Then we decide if it's good or bad. Feelings follow: more images, more ideas. It's a river of sorts, a strong one. But we aren't especially helped by it. The bear cubs mewing plaintively in high branches are good at first, but then bad, because nobody wants to mess with a riled up Momma bear and she must be around here somewhere. The fawn tracks are amazing - so delicate, so precious - but then a source of worry: did they make it back to their glade before the coy dogs came down from the hills to feed?

And so on. We all do this. We call it seeing and thinking and living. It feels natural and seems reasonable but it's a lot of work. And in the end it's quite painful. Creation asks nothing of us and yet we litter it with answer after answer. We are always so eager to inject our opinions and beliefs into life and it does not need any of it. Neither do we.

If we want to experience inner peace and real joy then we must begin with *how* we see: which is to say, how we make the world in which we believe we live. We must unlearn what we think we know about cause and effect.

> You see no neutral things because you have no neutral thoughts. It is always the thought that comes first, despite the temptation to believe that it is the other way around. This is not the way the world thinks, but you must learn that it is the way you think.

Thus, our focus begins to shift: we enter a sort of nebulous space, an interior space in which we do not analyze the bear cubs or the fawns or the floating ducks or the scent of honeysuckle or the neighbor and his cup of coffee coming over to talk.

Rather, we see *how* we see: the ground from which thought emerges, how thought operates, what it does vs. what we believe it does. This is not meditation in the sense of assuming certain postures and breathing methods. It is instead a heightened awareness, a giving of our attention. If it helps to invoke Jesus or the Holy Spirit to reach this space then we do it. When we ask for help, help is given, always in the form in which we can most readily accept it.

As we practice, our seeing becomes less and less invested in form, and more and more invested on simply discerning what is true from what is false: and this experience of discernment is entirely interior. It is devoted to the source, or cause, and not to mere effects.

> Whatever lies you may believe are of no concern to the miracle, which can heal any of them with equal ease. It makes no distinctions among misperceptions. Its sole concern is to distinguish between truth on the one hand, and error on the other.

You know, I think of my brothers and sisters often as I walk through the forest - the ones who are close to me in time and space, the ones who are not. I hold in mind our precious relationship as I watch the soft rays of the sun at dawn, push through the tangle of blackberry bushes ascending the hill, stop to gaze at fingerling trout darting through the pond's shallows. Such loveliness is almost unbearable! And yet I push past it to the thoughts that give rise to it all: and the Source, the "truth as God created it."

    That is where our minds are one. That is where - outside of time and space altogether - we give to each other equally, are blessed accordingly and find our way home together.

BEYOND WHAT CAN BE TAUGHT

One of the ways - perhaps *the* way - that the egoic self keeps us focused on separation from God (and not on atonement, not on remembering that we are one with God) is its insistence on finding and analyzing meaning. What is the meaning of life? The meaning of peace? Of conflict? Of the self? That is what judgment is: the search for, and categorization of, meaning.

This is not an insignificant observation. The human brain and psyche have evolved in such a way that the quest for meaning appears to have great value. We are all of us deeply attached to it. To even begin to detach from it is radical. To say that everything - from a lovely sunset to a Monet painting to a mushroom-shaped cloud on the horizon - is meaningless feels reckless and frightening.

We are sustained by our ideas about life: being a mother means this, being a husband means that, being a teacher means this, being a writer means that. Living in northern Europe has this meaning, living within such and such a tax bracket has that meaning. And so forth.

If we surrender all of that, what remains? It can feel Wile E. Coyote going full tilt, then skidding to a stop and seeing that he left solid ground twenty yards back.

It feels like falling. It feels like dying. And that is why we resist it.

Yet the attentive student sees quickly and early on that *A Course in Miracles* is bent on undoing meaning. It is not negotiable. Look at the *Introduction* to the text.

> The course does not aim at teaching the meaning of love, for that is beyond what can be taught. It does aim, however, at removing the blocks to the awareness of love's presence, which is your natural inheritance.

In other words, the course is not an intellectual exercise in defining love or the Holy Spirit or the trinity or the resurrection. Rather, it is a practical means by which we undo - remove - that which blocks our awareness of love. It aims for an experience, not words about experience. We are already good enough at talking about things and having ideas about things. Now we want to move beyond that into something that is new, something that is alive.

It is like the difference between designing a bridge based on an exhaustive study of the history of bridges and simply building a bridge. Our goal is to actually get to the other side - to do what needs to be done - not analyze the process from some metaphysical sideline.

The early lessons reinforce this emphasis on shifting away from the quest for meaning. Take a look, for example, at lessons one and four. The first asks us to consider that everything we perceive with our physical eyes is meaningless. The fourth adds our thoughts - which seem to be internal but are actually external - to the mix.

This can be a very destabilizing experience. When we begin to appreciate how deep-rooted our attachment to meaning is, the effort to release it can seem almost suicidal. No wonder the ego fights back, and no wonder we legitimize its resistance. This can go on for years. Lifetimes even.

Yet the course does not leave us at the abyss. Its objective is not to terrify or intimidate. Rather, it is to suggest - gently but firmly - that we are simply confused about meaning, and that as we willfully give attention to this confusion, then the confusion will clear and we will naturally be restored to wholeness.

That is the premise of the lines I quoted from the *Introduction*: we aren't analyzing love, we are facilitating an awareness of love. A deeply personal awareness. And lesson four is even more explicit.

The aim here is to train you in the first steps toward the goal of separating the meaningless from the meaningful. It is a first attempt in the long-range purpose of learning to see the meaningless as outside you, and the meaningful within.

What is the upshot of all this? It allows contact with what is essential about *A Course in Miracles*: its practical emphasis on undoing the separation through miracles. I am not called to an academic or intellectual experience, but to a healing experience that is outside the range of what I call my thoughts. It is outside the range of the brain and outside personal survival. It contemplates another level and another intelligence and other energies

This can seem very mysterious and mystical - and it is tempting to take refuge in poetic language about union with God and all of that - but it is really hard work. We are giving up - inch by inch, thought by thought, memory by memory - what we call life in favor of love and in favor of reality. It is beyond what can be taught. And it is only our willingness - not our understanding - that takes us there.

QUESTION: That doesn't sit right with me. The course is very intellectual. It is very logical. Parts of it are in iambic pentameter. Some of its ideas require time and energy to learn - like projection. So how can you say that my understanding doesn't matter?

ANSWER: I think maybe it is like riding a bike. If you think about it for a moment, that is an experience that we learn by doing. Somebody helps us, sure, but we have to actually be on the bike doing the work. And we are a little unsteady and wobbly, and we are probably going to get bumped and bruised a little, but we are going to be riding on our own. We are going to do it.

If you think about what is involved in biking – the physics of it – it is really insane. Just to maintain one's balance while turning and not losing track of traffic and direction and all of that – requires thousands and thousands of adjustments and calculations. The mathematics is astounding. But we don't do any of the math because we are just riding a bike. It is natural.

So I am suggesting that a similar principle might apply in terms of our practice of *A Course in Miracles*. We are reading it, and maybe reading this or that teacher, and we are picking up a lot of it but some of it is just sailing over our heads, and it's okay. That's the wobbly part. That's the falling down and getting back up part. But forgiveness is not intellectual or academic. Being kind is not a matter of having some wordy realization in the brain. That is not the level of Love and the level of Love is where the course is coming into application. That's where the change is taking place. We might notice it a little in the world and in our lives but that's just the after effects of thinking with Jesus and the Holy Spirit.

I think this happens to everyone who really applies themselves to studying and practicing *A Course in Miracles*. At some point you realize that you are getting it – you are more peaceful, more happy, more helpful – and it has nothing to do with you. You are not doing anything. It's being done through you. Your job is to just get out of the way of it. And somehow you learned that, and how to do it, and you are doing it. It's the same as with the bike. You are not doing all the math in order to make the turn, but you are making the turn.

Of course, we have to practice. I'm not suggesting we don't. But I am saying that placing emphasis on understanding can slow us down. The relevant understanding, if we want to use that word, happens at a level other than the level of mind. Things that don't make sense to the ego, to our basic understanding of how life works, are very pleasing to the spirit. That is where they are brought into application. There is a qualification at the beginning of the workbook that is very important: You don't have to believe in what these lessons teach to benefit from them. You just have to do them. So you know, we can relax our brains. Let them carry on but without giving them so much of our attention.

QUESTION: You use the word "other levels" and "another intelligence." Can you be more specific?

ANSWER: Well, we can keep it simple and say that there is the level of ego and its systems and constructs, which is where we are most of the time, and then there is the level of spirit which is abstract and creative and infinite.

When we have that moment I alluded to a moment ago – about realizing that Love is flowing through us, is being expressed through us, and that we are not responsible for it and are not directing it – then we are in touch with what I mean by another level. It is like we are being infused by something and so we turn to look at it: where is this infusion of energy or whatever coming from? How is this happening? And we discover that it's not hiding from us. It seems like it should be a secret or a mystery but it's not. So we start to explore that a little. We test it. Can I call on it? When I forget it's there, will it return if I remember it? How far back does it reach? Is anybody else here? Can I communicate at this level? How? All of it.

Again, it is just in the nature of exploring – of pushing a little at what we are experiencing and seeing what it yields. It is very hard to talk about using relative words. But you know, it is so much larger and more alive – more in motion – than anything else. It is like you go on vacation and have this amazing experience and then when you go home, you realize that you can still go on this vacation whenever you want. It slowly becomes more real than home.

I am butchering things a little with these metaphors, of course - "home" is probably confusing in this context – but I am trying to say that there are levels to perception and we can encounter them and explore them. We go into it and come back, go into it and come back but each time we come back we maybe stay away from it a little less. And soon enough we are redefining our idea of what "home" is to include this new space. Because the thing is, it isn't any different from us. It isn't alien.

QUESTION: And it's intelligent?

ANSWER: Yes. But to be clear, I don't mean intelligent in the way that our brains measure intelligence. I am not saying something like these levels of perception are separate entities with diplomas and advanced degrees and all that. Trees are intelligent. Flowers are intelligent. A river is intelligent. Can I say that? Would you agree? They know what they are. They are not sentient the way that a human is perhaps, but they are not confused. They are fully themselves and they fulfill their function. So I ask what is it that gives them their intelligence – that kind of intelligence? It is a sort of knowing without any alternative. A flower does not perceive choice. It simply manifests and expresses tulip or rose or bluet or what-have-you. The suggestion is that manifestation reflects intelligence – not perhaps as the brain understands it – but nonetheless intelligent. There is a kind of knowing. And these levels of perception that we are beginning to see and explore, they are informed by that intelligence too. It doesn't make mistakes. It doesn't indulge in choice. It knows. And its knowing is what makes it so peaceful and enlightening and so loving.

ON CHOOSING INNER PEACE

In a sense, inner peace is simply the absence of contingencies. Our happiness is no longer dependent on a certain arrangement of external circumstances. We make contact with the Source of peace, which is internal and capable of decision. We no longer confuse the application of the fundamental law of cause of effect.

In practical terms, we have to resolve to make inner peace the central fact of our lives. The world teaches us to value how much money we make, what our bodies look like, what we do with and to other bodies, what baubles and accoutrements we get for those bodies.

A Course in Miracles suggests that those values are misbegotten and altogether unworthy of a Son or Daughter of God.

Child of God, you were created to create
the good, the beautiful and the holy. Do
not forget this.

    But we do forget it, and thus condemn ourselves to the misery of the world and its bodies. We believe in them: we work hard to believe them. It's not the body that's the problem - the body itself is neutral - but rather our belief, our studied insistence, that they are real. It is that belief that hides the peace of God from us.
    Thus, we aren't called to refuse the body - to starve it or punish it – any more than we are called to glorify it. Rather, we simply want to see that we have made a decision to make the body and its world the central fact of our lives. We want to be clear that the role it plays in our lives is a choice that we have made. It is a decision.
    Why does that matter? Because when we reach the point of seeing a decision was made, we can begin to relate to that intelligence - that presence - that made (and makes) decisions.
    Thus, we begin to understand - dimly at first, but with increasing clarity and vigor - that a decision was made to dream. And so a decision can be made to wake up as well. The decision does not happen at the level of the body. It does not depend in any way upon what is external. We see the dream for what it is and we make another choice.

> The body's serial adventures, from the
> time of birth to dying are the theme of
> every dream the world has ever had . . .

> the dream has but one purpose, taught in
> many ways. This single lesson does it try
> to teach again, and still again, and yet
> once more; that it is cause and not effect.
> And you are its effect, and cannot be its
> cause.

That which makes decisions is a cause. It is not an effect. What we are in truth is an effect only of the Love that is God. Beyond that, we are cause, creating as we were created, because that is Love's will: that it extend itself infinitely and without qualification or condition.

Thus, salvation becomes the recognition that choice is possible and that - having chosen wrongly - we can "choose again."

> You always choose between your weakness and the strength of Christ in you.
> And what you choose is what you think is
> real. Simply by never using weakness to
> direct your actions, you have given it no
> power. And the light of Christ in you is
> given charge of everything you do. For
> you have brought your weakness to Him,
> and He has given you His strength instead.

Inner peace is the result of accepting responsibility for peace. When we stop looking for it where it is not, we will find it. Why? Because it is the natural consequence of understanding the law of cause and effect. In truth, peace is as simple as deciding it is what we want. It's not hiding; rather we are simply in denial about our power to choose it.

Thus, the question is always this: are we ready to be peaceful? Are we ready to be happy? And if not now, when?

A LOVING YES

    I woke from terrifying dreams a little before 5 a.m. and stumbled outside with the dog. Stars were shooting across the sky. I know better than to translate them into signs of God's favor. We headed east toward black hills, past fields still clumped with snow, into the darker forest. Now and then I would stop and look up: streams of light criss-crossing space, rangeless and open, like a shoreless ocean, rich, flowing and eternal.

    I prayed as we walked, which is to say that I gave attention as we walked, ever longing for the peace that flowers when I can allow God to simply be present. It is not easy. It is simple, but not easy. People were dying in my dream and I watched them suffer. It was not clear that my fate was not going to be the same. Do you know how it is, when the bad dreams are so real you wake up sweating and trembling? And when you realize it was just a dream, you think, "where did *that* come from?"

How I hate having a mind that can create such anguish and hurt! And yet . . .

A Course in Miracles challenges me to release the world. The story of this life - its bad dreams, its fleeting pleasures, its apparent struggles for money, for grace, for love, for justice - was written long ago. The question is not whether I can do anything about it now, but rather with whom I watch it unfold. Does that make sense? We are not doing anything as we understand doing. We are simply making space for the presence of the Holy One. The rest is simply allowing it all to be undone. There is nothing else.

And yet . . .

The ego – the false self with whom we navigate this painful illusion called life in the world - fosters only the doomed sense that one cannot ever escape. It is folly to even try, though wishing for something better - a sort of taunt, really - is always okay. The Holy Spirit on the other hand - opposite of the egoic self in every way - gently shines the many illusions away, at whatever pace and to whatever degree we can handle offering it a loving yes.

Willingness is a kind of affirmation. It is like saying, "yes. I see that I cannot do this all on my own. I see that what I think I am is broken and incapable of love. Yes, I will avail myself of resources that are holy and impeccable. Yes."

To say yes is to be open. To say yes in this way is to confirm that we believe in a love that transcends the agony and conflict inherent in duality and thus inherent in the world. It opens up that space in which God is - in which Love is - and we are free of thought, free of consequence altogether.

The only question we ever need to answer is: whose Kingdom is the world for you today? Does it belong to the ego? Or to God?

A few weeks ago I surfed a particularly difficult and painful time. It passed. This happens. The closer we come to Christ, the more frantic and even violent the ego's defenses become. You can feel as if you cursed - as if you are the living embodiment of all dysfunction and insanity. Let it be, if you can. It only gets worse when we fight it. The ego is tricky and its defense systems are subtle. If it can't get its way screaming and kicking, then it will try another route. It will feign logic or compassion. It will can seem so reasonable. It allows a little peace in and so we stop fighting. We think, "I did it. I got it. I beat the ego by embracing Jesus."

Maybe. But maybe not, too.

It is a dangerous game of balance the ego plays, especially once we've had a taste of the real peace offered by turning to the Holy Spirit. The ego wants us miserable and then dead but it has to be careful. If the misery and fear become too much we might turn altogether to the One who can show us the better way. We might learn that the ego is simply an idea we can release the way late summer milkweed release their tendril seeds . . .

It can happen that way. It *does* happen that way.

I have learned in recent months that the necessary undoing - the revelation of Truth - is vast. My penchant for conflict - for indulging the ego - is deep-rooted and ugly. It's wily like a fox. Nightmares abound lately, even as my day-to-day waking life subsides into manageability. How do we get off the roller-coaster?

"There is no roller coaster," Jesus says patiently, for the ten thousandth time since we believe we climbed on board. "It ends when you say it ends."

"Don't be a fool," whispers the ego. "This ride is all there is and you know it."

So it goes. You can't fight it. You don't want to join it. So you trudge. This is how it is.

The dog and I headed back just as the sky was beginning to soften with light, the star slowly dimming. I made tea, sat by the window, then knelt suddenly to pray. "Help me," I said. "Just help me. Please."

I want to tell you that Jesus rode in on a beam of light so golden and strong that I was blinded. Or that he sent an angel with flowing locks and a good sense of humor. But that isn't how it works for me. However, I did notice that suddenly I could look at the dream images that had woken me in terror and not feel overwhelmed by them. They seemed one-dimensional. Another chapter in the ego's grim narrative but not more than that. Not greater than God.

So I could function again. I sat down and wrote for a couple of hours. When the kids got up, I made pancakes. Life went on.

I won't lie to you. I have come through considerable darkness and I am not going to turn back. I may stumble and I may complain but I am not returning. I might fall for the illusions now and again, but I am intent now on remembering to look beyond them with the Teacher who will undo them. I ask for help and accept it when it arrives. It's not easy. I often feel that I am walking in darkness. There is no light anywhere and yet for some reason my feet always seem to step on solid ground. Do you know what I am saying? You sense that you are being held, or guided, or maybe even lifted.

For a long time I understood this writing this way to be all about me - my learning, my edification, my glory. But maybe I am wrong. Maybe it's about you. Maybe you, reading this right now - whatever time it is, wherever you are- are blessing me. Maybe you are the one doing the lifting.

So maybe all I need to say is thank you. Thank you. Thank you. *Thank you.*

One or Two Steps Only

NOTES

Material quoted from A Course in Miracles is taken from versions which are in the Public Domain.

For more information about ACIM, please visit acim.org.

Some of the poems were published in assorted and sundry publications over the years. Grateful acknowledgement is hereby made.

ABOUT ME

I live and write in New England. It is both my home and - once you settle certain ideas about Oneness and God into its landscape - my theme. Writers like Emily Dickinson, Robert Frost, Jonathan Edwards and Henry Thoreau paved the way for my humble - quite humble, really - efforts. My poems, reportage, essays, op-eds and short stories have appeared in hundreds of journals and magazines over the years, including Yankee Magazine, Rattle, AmericanStyle, The Bark, Modern Haiku and others. I've been a lawyer, a music therapist, a reporter, an English professor, a political blogger and a stay-at-home Dad. Mostly I write about atonement - the experience of undoing our mutual separation from God in the interest of inner peace and joy. *A Course in Miracles* is my spiritual path, for lack of a better word, and I'm especially partial to Tara Singh's take on it. Krishnamurti and David Bohm have helped considerably as well. I'm a hobo at heart but happy, against what once seemed like long odds.

Come visit: seanreagan.com

Printed in Great Britain
by Amazon